sex and candy

Emma Bray

chapter
one

Ace

I **TAKE** a sip of the subpar whiskey in front of me and grimace at the taste as I glance down at my Rolex. Fucker's late.

I drum my fingers on the table in irritation, keenly reminded of why I never let anyone pick meeting locations. You never know what kind of seedy joint they're going to want to meet up in or if they'll even show up at all.

I knew better than to let MacHay dictate the terms of this meeting, but I went against my better instincts and did it anyway. Simply because the man has proven so difficult to get in touch with. I'm regretting ever shaking his hand in the first place, and if I wasn't beholden to hold up my end of the bargain, I'd say fuck it and bail on this here and now.

Oh, well. You live and learn, right?

I'm tempted to do it anyway and am actually moving to slip out of my booth when the stage lights up and a hush falls over the audience.

I don't know what causes me to pause and sit back down. It's probably just going to be another subpar dancer like all the other ones that have been staggering around on the stage all night.

Maybe it's the pregnant pause of anticipation that seems to fall over the entire room.

I don't know.

But when the tiniest little angel I've ever seen steps on stage, time itself seems to stop.

Her skin glows ivory under the stage light. She has on a lacy white number, some sort of bustier, lacy panties, and white stockings. The look is topped off with fire engine red heels that match the paint on her lips. Long lashes frame light brown eyes that look too big and luminous for her little heart-shaped face. Long blonde hair like spun gold falls in glorious waves all the way down to an impossibly tiny waist that I know I could cup in my two hands. My breath catches in my throat. My god, she looks like a porcelain doll come to life.

But what most arrests me is the look in her eyes. For a split second when she first steps out on stage, her wide eyes are soulfully sad, so much so that they seem to take my breath away.

They seem to mirror all the tragedy in the world in their depths.

But then it's gone in the blink of an eye as she smiles, a dazzling, heart-wrenching smile that makes me instantly jealous. I'm irrationally upset that's she's gracing this roomful of men with that smile—that smile that I suddenly know deep down in my soul is meant to be only mine.

Mine.

Sultry music begins to play, and she begins to dance, gently swaying her hips as she flirts with the strip pole.

I'm gripping the edge of the table so tightly I'm surprised the wood doesn't break underneath my palms. I swear to God if one piece of clothing comes off her body I won't be able to stop myself from rushing up on that stage and covering her from prying eyes.

I'm aware that my reaction is insane. I don't know anything about this girl, but I can't stop the surge of possessive protectiveness that rages inside me at the thought of all these men seeing her so scantily clad like this.

What the fuck is she doing? Doesn't she know she's an angel? Doesn't she know she doesn't belong in here with all these devils?

I grit my teeth when she suddenly flings herself on the pole and begins to do a series of complicated flips and turns. The men roar and whistle and cheer, and I'd bet my last million half the fuckers in this place have a boner right now imagining her little body writhing on their laps like she is on that pole.

The thought fills me with murderous rage.

I'm so distracted by it that I don't even notice when MacHay finally takes his seat across from me until he chuckles and comments, "It's your first time witnessing the wonder that is Candy, huh?"

"What?" I bark at him, never tearing my eyes away from the beauty up on the stage. I feel like I won't be able to rest until her set is over and she's safely back behind that stage curtain where she belongs out of sight of lascivious male eyes.

He juts his chin out at the stage. "Candy. She's the feature dancer here." I spare a sideways glance at him out of the corner of my eye. He takes a sip of his drink and motions toward the stage with it, "And you can see why. Not only is she the prettiest one out of the bunch, but she's also the youngest and the one with the most skill. Consequently, she's the one Dan hoards to himself like the finest treasure. You can pay for a little extra with the other dancers, if you know what I mean, but Dan won't let anyone near Candy for no amount of money."

I frown, though I can't help feeling some sort of relief at the thought that Candy isn't being prostituted out. I can barely stomach the thought of all these men's eyes on her, much less their hands.

"So," MacHay rubs his hands together eagerly as Candy's show ends and she leaves the stage. I notice how she doesn't scramble to pick up any of the money thrown on the stage for her like all the dancers before her did. She walks coolly off the stage without even a backward glance at all the men she now holds in her thrall. "You really to get down to business?" MacHay interrupts my thoughts.

I scowl at him. The fucker keeps me waiting all the time, and then he shows up and expects me to cater to him. He can fucking wait now.

I level him with a cool stare before I stand from the booth and pull out my phone. "I have something to attend to first. If you want to see any part of this partnership go forward, you'll be sitting right here waiting for me when I get back."

He frowns and looks like he wants to say something,

but one look at my tight jawline and he obviously thinks better of it, giving a curt nod of understanding instead. Yeah, he knows he fucked up.

I step out of earshot and call my head of security.

"Yeah, James? Get me everything you can on a dancer at the club on Sixth. Pronto. I want everything within the next thirty minutes. Goes by the name of Candy..."

Candy

I frown as I look at the girl in the mirror. I hardly recognize myself, and my chest squeezes when I think of what my mom would think if she could see me now.

I know she'd be disappointed to find me here dancing in Dan's club rather than realizing my full potential as a gymnast.

I grit my teeth when I remind myself that this isn't entirely my fault, though. If she hadn't married the slimy fucker, I might not be in this situation.

As soon as Mom died, Dan made it perfectly clear that his duty to me was over. He never was much of a father figure, and he was a shitty stepfather at that. He never tried to touch me, but that didn't stop him from leering at me like a rabid dog.

I never got what my mom saw in him.

With her out of the way and me eighteen, he told me in no uncertain terms that I wasn't going to be his charity case, that I would have to earn my keep like anyone else.

So, that's how I ended up putting all my gymnastics skills to waste on a strip pole. The only decent thing Dan's ever done for me is ensure no one messes with me. None of the guys from the club are allowed to touch—much less proposition—me.

I'm the feature performer. You can look but not touch, and I suppose that's the most I can ask for in this world.

Somehow, I live in this seedy sex den and have managed to hang on to my virginity. It's the one thing that's still mine, and I have no intention of giving it up any time soon.

I don't know if Dan knows I'm a virgin or not, but I'm guessing not. Otherwise, he'd have surely found a way to capitalize on it by now. Probably sell me off to the highest bidder.

At first, I kept telling myself that I would only do this for a little while, that I would save up enough money to go out on my own and get my own place and I'd get back to my dream of being a gymnast.

But Dan quickly stripped me of that illusion when

he made it clear that any tips I get go to him—not me. I don't get to keep a dime of what I make in this club. It all goes to my room and board and upkeep.

I'm effectively trapped, and it sucks because half of me hates my mom for what she left me with. And that makes me feel guilty. How horrible of a person do you have to be to hate your dead mother? I still love her, but I hate what she did to me.

It's not her fault she got breast cancer and died, but it is her fault she married Dan and left her young daughter with the sleezeball instead of any sort of inheritance or even a decent man who would make sure she gets a halfway decent start in this world.

It's complicated as fuck and leaves me feeling all knotted up inside, so I try not to think about it.

I push my hair back from my face and sigh before I get up and walk out to the front. After performing, we're required to hit the floor and help serve drinks, let the men get a closer look at us so they're prompted to drink more and keep coming back if they feel like they know us.

I'm not on the floor for two minutes when I feel eyes boring into me. Of course, I'm being stared at from all sides. I'm used to having eyes on me. But that's not what this is.

This is...more.

My eyes flit around the room, searching for the source of the heat on my body.

And then they slam right into it.

Golden eyes that seem to mirror the brightness of the sun. They're blazing into me from across the room. Those eyes that seem to burn more intensely than the brightest star are held within a handsome face that looks like it belongs on the cover of a men's magazine. The man's jawline is straight and lined with stubble, but not the kind of stubble that says he's lazy. No, it's the kind of stubble that somehow still manages to look stylish and sexy and even a little bit dangerous.

His hair is dark and just long enough on the top that I'm sure women love to run their fingers through it.

He's tall, and I can see his muscles even through the suit he wears. Everything about him exudes power, and warning bells are already going off in my head before he ever starts making his way over to where I'm carrying a tray of drinks.

I turn on my little red heels and start walking away from him, my heart picking up at the determined look I saw in his eyes before turning my back on him. I don't know what it is about the man that has me wanting to both draw closer to him and run far away from him, but I'm going with the latter instinct and trying to put as much distance between us as possible.

A man that looks that big and powerful in a place like this with his sights set on me can't possibly spell anything good for me.

Never mind that he just might be the most handsome man I've ever seen. Wasn't Lucifer God's most beautiful angel? And yeah, look how that turned out.

I almost make it all the way to the back when a deep voice, smooth as velvet skates over my ear.

"Where you rushing off to in such a hurry, dollface?"

I can't stop the involuntary shiver that wracks my frame at that voice and the feeling of it tickling across my skin. He's standing entirely too close to me.

I set the tray of drinks I'm holding down on the bar since my hands are trembling and I don't want to chance spilling them and making a huge fool out of myself.

I turn around to face him, taking a few steps back, a frown already fixed on my face. I just need to shoot him down really quick, and then I can get on with my night.

"That's really none of your business," I smile up at him sweetly, though my voice is dripping with condescension.

He blinks in obvious surprise at my snarky tone, but he's not deterred.

Instead, a wide grin overtakes his face, and he chuckles.

"Feisty. I like that."

My cheeks burn, and I pivot on my heel to walk away from him, but a gentle hand on my bare shoulder stops me.

I suck in a breath as sparks shoot along my skin where his flesh meets mine. His touch is hot and heavy. I jerk back from him like I've been singed, whirling around to glare daggers at him. "Don't touch me," I hiss at him.

He holds his hands up in surrender, though the heated look in his gaze says he's anything but sorry.

"Look, I have a proposition for you," he states.

My eyebrows shoot up to my hairline as I look up at him incredulously. "You must be new here. I'm not one of the girls you can proposition. If I tell Dan what you even suggested, he'll have you thrown out of here on your ass so fast your head will spin."

He stares at me for a tick before he lowers his hands and tucks them into his pockets, shaking his head. "Not that kind of proposition. Jesus."

I cross my arms and level him with a look.

His eyes wander over my face. "I want to offer to get you out of here," he says.

I stare at him a moment before I allow a humorless laugh to burst out of me.

He doesn't see the humor in the situation, though. He just stands there staring down at me.

I finally scoff at him, "Let me guess. You think I'm too pretty and too good for this place, so you want to save me? Take me far away from here, and I'll be indebted to you for the rest of my life? No thanks," I shake my head. "I'm not trading one prison for another. The devil you know and all that, you know?" I raise a mocking brow at him. All us dancers have heard this all before from men who promise to take us away from here, marry us, love us, treat us right. The dumb ones believe them and run off with dreams of rainbows in their eyes only to find themselves worse off than ever before.

Those of us who have half a brain—like me—see through that bullshit for what it is: pipe dreams.

The man's jaw hardens. He doesn't like being mocked.

"I'm not offering to be your savior. I'm offering you a job, *Candace*. A chance at something better."

My head snaps up at his use of my real name. No one from the club knows my real name. My cheeks heat, and I narrow my eyes at him. "How do you know my name?"

He shrugs. "Candy, Candace. It's not hard to put two and two together. Lucky guess." He raises an eyebrow at me. I know he's lying. It wasn't a lucky guess. Somehow this man knows more about me than he's letting on, and that knowledge is unsettling.

I give him a scathing look. "And who are you?"

He looks unfazed by my derision. "Ace," he answers back simply.

I should turn around and walk away from him right now, but something holds me back. I huff and cross my arms over my chest again. To his credit, I haven't seen his eyes stray from my face the whole time we've been talking. My damned curiosity is getting the better of me. "What kind of job?" I ask suspiciously.

He smiles a slow grin that ends in him flashing a million-dollar smile that I'm sure has girls wetting their panties all over the country. "I need a personal assistant. Someone to help me with my schedule and other menial tasks. Sort my office. That sort of thing. Nothing too demanding."

"And you think I look like the kind of girl who'd be good at that sort of thing?" I snort.

He levels me a look that lets me know he doesn't appreciate my self-deprecation. "Yes, I do. I think there's much more to you than meets the eye. Candace."

He tacks my name onto the end of his statement like a caress, his tongue stroking each syllable. I try to ignore the involuntary shiver that wants to go through me at the way he says my name, like he's not just saying it. He's *tasting* it.

"And what if there's not?" I thrust my chin up at

him. "What if what you see is what you get? What if I like working here?"

His tongue slowly licks along his bottom lip, and I feel my face flush at the erotic nature of the move. "You and I both know that's not true," he states with absolute certainty.

Damn him. Damn him for looking so handsome. Damn him for seeing right through me.

Damn him for making me hope.

I tap my foot as I consider. Can I really do this? Can I really leave here and go work for him? Have a chance at something better than this shitty club?

He sees the moment I actually start considering his offer, and he latches onto it. "I guarantee I'll pay you more than you've ever made here, and you'll never have to dance half naked on a pole again."

The way he says that—*you'll never have to dance half naked on a pole again*—fills me with shame. And then the hopelessness of my situation swarms over me again.

"It doesn't matter," I state flatly. "Dan will never let me leave."

He smiles slowly, triumph lighting his eyes. "Just leave Dan to me."

chapter
two

Ace

SHE'S TOO MOTHERFUCKING PRETTY for words.

And she's mine.

All mine.

Well, she doesn't know that yet. But she will.

Soon.

I sit back in my desk chair and run my thumb over my bottom lip as I watch her type away at the computer in front of her. I had a desk set up for her in here with me so I could keep an eye on her. I've given her some menial tasks to do. Just some busy work to make her feel useful like she's really earning her keep, but I don't really need her help.

Hell, if I thought she'd allow it, I wouldn't have her doing anything but just sitting there looking pretty and keeping me company.

But I already know Candace is too prideful to accept anything less than what she perceives as a real job.

It was hard enough convincing her to stay here in my home as part of her room and board. When she accepted the position as my assistant, she no doubt pictured us working in an office setting. And while I do have an actual office, there's no way in hell I'm sharing her.

No, I want her all to myself. All day, every day.

She didn't anticipate my cozy home office that throws the two of us together in this intimate situation.

But of course that's exactly what I'd had in mind all along.

Her piece of shit stepfather was a piece of cake to buy off. Technically, I didn't have to buy him off, but it just made my life a hell of a lot easier to pay the guy off, essentially "buying" Candy from him than to have to deal with him and his goons constantly coming after her.

Candace doesn't ever need to know that, though. Something tells me she wouldn't take kindly to the knowledge that I'd essentially paid for her.

So, I don't plan on her ever finding that out. Besides,

I don't view her that way, as something to be bought and sold. And I don't ever want her to think I think so little of her.

On the contrary, I think the world of her. So much so that I've shamelessly finagled everything to where she can be sitting here with me all day long.

No matter that she scowls every time she looks up and finds my gaze on her.

She's still as prickly as a porcupine when it comes to me, but that's okay. I'm a patient man.

And I have all the time in the world to woo my little girl. I might be thirty, but she's only eighteen. Her attitude makes her seem much older than that, though. I have to remember that she's become somewhat jaded by the environment she's been working in, and it'll take her time to trust me.

My eyes rove over her now. She's looking down at the papers on the desk in front of her as her fingers fly over the keys, entering the data into the computer. Part of her blonde hair falls over the front of her shoulder, and she mindlessly pushes it back behind her so that it cascades down her back in rustle of shiny waves. On another woman, the move would look calculated, but with her, it's completely innocent.

She's totally unaware of what she's doing.

She bites her lip in concentration, and my eyes hone

in on the puffy flesh. Her nibbling on it is causing all the blood to rush to it, staining it cherry red instead of its natural rosy pink.

I have to bite back a groan as all the blood in my body rushes south to my cock.

Christ, she looks so motherfucking sweet. I can't help thinking that her nickname is appropriate. I guaran-fucking-tee she tastes just like candy.

She feels me studying her. Her eyes flick up and catch me watching her, and she frowns.

"Stop it," she says.

I can't stop the grin that spreads across my face at her attention.

"Stop what, dollface?"

Her scowl only deepens at my pet name for her.

"Stop staring at me like..." she trails off, her face reddening.

My grin widens, and I can't stop the chuckle that rumbles up out of my chest. "Like what, doll?"

Her cheeks are stained pink, and she huffs, going back to her typing.

I can't let it go, though. She's too much fun to toy with. Plus, she's so fucking beautiful when she's all pissed and flustered. It doesn't matter that she's wearing jeans and an oversized T-shirt. She's just as beautiful in casual wear as she was in the lingerie she was wearing the night I met her at her stepfather's club.

"Go on. Finish that thought," I press her.

She presses her lips together, and I laugh, goading her.

She finally snaps angry eyes up to me and hisses, "Like you want to eat me or something."

I'm so shocked I throw my head back and boom with laughter.

When I finally get myself under control enough to look at her without tears rolling down my face, I take in her flushed countenance. I can't help teasing her some more.

"Oh, but I love sweet things," I tell her, "especially candy." My cock leaps within my slacks when I see the blush deepen on her cheeks.

"You're incorrigible," she mutters as she goes back to typing, trying her best to ignore me.

I decide I've teased her enough for one day and leave her be. It's not that I don't want to play with her some more. It's that I don't know how much more I can take without pouncing on her.

Having her sitting in the same room as me day in and day out looking so fucking delectable is giving me a permanent case of blue balls, and I don't know how much longer I can hold off on touching her. I'm a patient man, but even I have my limits, and Candace is the most tempting thing I've ever seen in my mother-fucking life.

When I finally get my cock somewhat under control, I leave the room.

Before I forget that I'm trying to be patient with her and throw her on my desk to feast on her.

Candy

I begrudgingly have to admit that I'm thankful Ace noticed me in the club that night and offered me this job. It's a relief to not have to dance in front of leering eyes knowing the lecherous thoughts in all their heads.

All I have to deal with now is one man. A man who's being surprisingly respectful despite the way he looks at me.

I'd be an idiot not to see the way Ace looks at me. He desires me. It's obvious. I'm sure that's the only reason he gave me this job.

But he hasn't tried to force himself on me, and I'm thankful for that.

At least, I think I am.

Okay, so the man is gorgeous. I'd have to be blind

not to notice that. And he's so polished and well put-together. Even though he works in an office in his home, he wears slacks and a button-up shirt every day. But it doesn't make him look uptight or stuffy. He still carries this powerful, almost dangerous aura about him. Maybe it's the way he wears his shirt with a few buttons open at the top and the sleeves rolled up. Like he's saying fuck you to convention. He's wearing the typical businessman clothing, but he's doing it his way.

Yet I feel safe with him. I halfway think he wears such nice clothes just because he knows how mouthwatering he looks in those clothes.

He doesn't require me to dress up, though, and I don't. I dress casual in jeans and simple tees every day. I certainly don't want to look like I'm trying to too hard and give him the wrong idea.

It doesn't seem to matter what I wear, though. That doesn't keep the man's eyes from devouring me whole every time we're in the same room together, which is pretty much all the time.

And as much as I hate to admit it, I'm starting to trust him.

He's been as good as his word, giving me a job and place to live along with food. And all without asking for anything shady in return. He hasn't so much as laid a finger on me.

I can't help but feel grateful to the person who helped me get away from Dan and his hellhole. Now, I might actually have a chance at saving up money and taking up gymnastics again. Maybe I can eventually start my own studio and teach. It's actually a very real possibility with how much Ace pays me.

I stretch and flip on my bedside lamp, my tummy growling. I didn't eat much at dinner. I'm not shy or anything, but it's hard to make yourself eat when you have a predator staring at you from the other end of the table, looking at you like *you're* his next meal rather than the food on the plate in front of him.

I fling back the covers and get out of bed to head down to the kitchen for a snack.

It's late, so I don't expect Ace to be up. When I walk past his office and see light coming from underneath the door, I pause.

I don't know what possesses me to do it, but I push open the door, my curiosity getting the best of me once again.

And what I see almost floors me.

Ace is standing by his desk, looking down at something.

While he jacks off.

My mouth falls open as I take in the image of his

powerful body stroking that thick column of flesh between his legs.

He's not wearing a shirt, so I can see the muscles in his chest and arms flexing with every movement. I'm surprised when I see a tribal band tattoo around the top of his right bicep, though why I'm surprised I don't know. Ace is totally the type to have a tattoo as another fuck you to convention.

All he's wearing are workout shorts, and he has them pulled down just enough to free his jutting cock to his ministrations.

I knew he was muscular, but nothing could have prepared me for the sight of his bare chest or the length and girth of just what he's packing between his thighs. I might be a virgin, but I've seen a man's cock before. It's hard not to when you work in the kind of place I worked in.

I've never seen one as impressive as Ace's before, though. Impressive is actually never a term I thought I'd apply to the male anatomy. Men were always one and the same to me. Disgusting pervs I had to perform for in order to keep a roof over my head and food in my belly.

But Ace has demolished all those preconceived notions I had. First, by offering me a job and a chance at a better life. Second, at not forcing himself on me. And now with the view of his god-like body. I've never been very religious, but I'm tempted to fall to my knees and actually begin worshipping him.

That's how perfect he looks.

My eyes follow his line of sight to see what he's looking at, and I can't help the gasp that escapes my throat when I see that it's a picture of...me.

It's not even a very racy photo. It's not like it's a picture of me wearing scanty lingerie on the pole back at the club.

It's just a picture of my face. A headshot that he must have discreetly taken some time since I've been here working for him because my eyes aren't focused on the camera. I'm looking off in the distance, probably at the computer screen.

His eyes snap up when he hears me gasp, but he never stops his stroking. His hand is still flying over that swollen flesh, only now instead of his concentration being on the photo in front of him, he's staring right at me.

My cheeks heat as his eyes bore directly into mine with more intensity than I've ever seen on his face. His golden eyes seem to glow as he stares right into my eyes.

I bite my lip nervously. God, I should leave, but I'm frozen to this spot, unable to tear my eyes away from his.

His eyes darken, and he lets out a guttural groan when I release my lip from my teeth. He throws his head back and cants his hip forward, thrusting into his hand. White liquid spurts from the tip, the thick ropes shooting up like a fountain.

And all I can do is stand there and watch in amazement, my face still flushed over the knowledge that it wasn't even my body that got him that way, but my face.

When I finally drag my eyes back up to his face, his steady gaze is on me. He doesn't look embarrassed or apologetic at all. His cock is still half hard, and he's staring at me intently, the desire still obvious on his face.

I can't breathe for a second as I hold his golden gaze. I vaguely notice that I'm aching and wet between my legs, and my face burns brighter because of it.

Ace continues to stare at me. It's as if we're at a pivotal moment. That gaze seems to dare me to take one step toward him. Part of me wants to just to find out what will happen.

But that other part of me that's a coward has me taking a step back from him instead.

I think I see a flicker of disappointment in his eyes, but I don't stick around to find out.

I turn on my heel and run back to my room, all thoughts of food forgotten. I'm suddenly not hungry anymore.

At least not for food...

chapter
three

Ace

CANDACE CAN HARDLY LOOK at me today. And I guess it's really no wonder when she caught me jacking off to a picture of her face.

And what did I do when I got caught? Did I stop and look ashamed like any halfway decent man would?

No, I kept fucking going, the churning in my balls only increasing at getting caught by the object of my obsession. Masturbating myself right in front of her, relishing at the shocked look on her face, the way her mouth fell open in a silent "o."

Imagining myself coming all in that sweet little mouth, smearing my seed all over those puffy pink lips.

Looking at those hard little nipples poking out through that tank top that was so damn near see through I could almost see the dusky rose of her aureolas.

The way she pressed her thighs together, letting me know that little clit of hers was swollen and throbbing at the sight of me stroking my cock. The thought that her pussy was juicy and wet watching me.

That she was actually very turned on by what she saw...

Fuck me.

Is it any wonder I came like a fucking geyser?

Considering the current state of things, coming right in front of her like that might not have been my best move.

But fuck if I could have stopped myself when she was right there in the flesh looking too delectable for words.

She always looks too damn good.

Like right now. I'm having to fight everything inside me to keep my hands off her.

She's like the most forbidden candy and I'm an addict with a serious sweet tooth.

I want to eat her.

She knows it too.

She feels my eyes on her and looks up at me, her face flushing crimson.

Damn if that doesn't make me want her more.

And as much as my sadistic ass is kind of enjoying her discomfort, I also want to clear the air.

I don't want her to be afraid of me. Just the thought has my chest tightening up.

"So, about last night..." I begin.

Her fingers fumble over the keys, and, if possible, her face turns an even brighter shade of red.

She glances up at me before looking back at the computer screen. "Um," she stammers. "I'm sorry. I didn't mean to walk in on you."

I frown. "You shouldn't be the one apologizing, Candace. You didn't do anything wrong. I'm the one who's sorry. Sorry if I made you uncomfortable, that is," I clarify. Hell no, I'm not sorry for busting a load while looking at her pretty face, but I am remorseful that she doesn't feel comfortable around me now.

She peeks up at me again. "What makes you think you made me uncomfortable?"

I bark out a laugh before raising a knowing eyebrow at her. "Maybe the fact that you can't even look me in the eye today and that you've barely spoken two words to me."

She bites her lip, and I feel my cock hardening within my pants.

Fuck...

Focus man, I have to remind myself.

I clear my throat. "Anyway, I just want you to know that I would never try to force you to do anything. I don't want you to be afraid of anything like that. You're safe here with me."

She's still looking at the computer screen when she licks her lips. Damn, this girl is going to kill me with those fucking lips alone.

"I'm not afraid," she says softly, finally meeting my eyes.

I study her for a moment, considering how honest I want to be. "But I won't lie," I finally confess solemnly. "I'm a man, and it's obvious I desire you. You're fucking beautiful, and I honestly don't think I've ever wanted anyone the way I want you." My voice comes out gravelly at the end. But there. I've laid all my cards on the table.

She looks like she might say something, but then she thinks better of it, bites her lip again, and then gives a curt nod.

Fuck it. Might as well get it all out.

"And one day when you're ready, I'm going to make you mine," I can't help adding.

Her mouth falls open, but I don't give her a chance

to respond. I stand and leave the room to hit the gym before I go ahead and make good on that promise whether she's ready or not.

▭

Candy

And one day when you're ready, I'm going to make you mine.

Who does that? I mean seriously? Who drops that kind of statement and then just walks out of the room all nonchalantly?

I sit there with my mouth gaping open for all of two seconds before fury overtakes me.

I slam my mouth shut and push back from the computer, intention in my every movement.

Just who the fuck does Ace think he is? He's had my emotions in a whirlwind ever since I came here. I'm always on edge, knowing what he wants from me yet *not knowing* what he wants from me.

He's always confusing me at every turn.

Studiously not touching me yet staring at me like I'm a juicy steak every second of the day. Being the perfect gentleman in action, but then his eyes are full of unspoken promises.

Jacking off to a picture of my face and then staring me right in the eyes as he comes, looking sexier than sin.

Letting me squirm and feel uncomfortable all day and then dropping a bomb like that and just walking out.

No. Just no. I am not going to play these little games anymore.

I go storming through the house to Ace's gym. Somehow I know that's where he's at. He tends to go there multiple times throughout the day. As if the man isn't sexy enough, he just can't help building his physique.

My mouth goes dry when I find him stripped down to his boxer briefs, his button-up shirt and slacks discarded on the floor.

He's lifting weights, every muscle in his chest and arms bulging with exertion.

He must sense me come in because he exhales a breath and sits the bar back in its holder before sitting up.

I shake my head as if to mentally clear the fog that's threatening to descend over me at the sight of Ace's powerful-looking body. Goodness, his thighs are like cannons, his abs defined. There's not an ounce of fat on the man.

And that somehow manages to just piss me off even more.

"What the hell was that?" I snap at him.

He doesn't even pretend to not know what I'm talking about. Instead, he lets out an exasperated sigh before he says very slowly, "Candace, not right now."

I cross my arms over my chest and glare at him. "Yes, I think right now. You wanted to talk about this, so let's talk."

He doesn't say anything. He just shoots me a looked filled with warning before he stands and turns to walk away from me.

And that just fucking infuriates me. I ignore the obvious warning he was giving me and fly after him, my hand reaching out to touch his shoulder—to do what, I'm not entirely sure. Spin him around and make him face me?

It doesn't matter what my intentions were, though, because as soon as my fingers touch his skin, Ace snaps.

He whirls around to face me and has me backed up against the wall in two point five seconds—so fast I can barely register what happened until I'm looking up at his face just inches from mine, my heart pounding in my chest.

His hands are against the wall on either side of my head, effectively trapping me in. His minty breath fans over my lips as he speaks a hair's breath from me. "I warned you, little Candy."

And then he kisses me, his lips crashing down onto mine brutally.

It's like I've been doused in flames. Fire is suddenly licking at every nerve ending in my body.

He expertly parts my mouth and slips his tongue inside, instantly seeking mine out and twining with it.

And damn me, but I melt against him, my hands on his hard chest. He places his own hands atop mine and holds me there while his mouth plunders mine like he's a pirate searching for treasure.

When his lips finally leave mine, they move across my jaw and down my neck, branding me with every hot touch.

He keeps my hands captured against his chest with one of his own, but he begins to explore with his other hand.

When he cups my breast and runs his thumb over my hardened peak, I can't stop the whimper that leaves my lips.

"Fuck, yes, baby," he whispers against my neck before he bites down on it and sucks, marking me.

I feel moisture pooling between my thighs, and

there's an insistent throbbing that has me slamming my legs together to try to ease the ache.

"Motherfucker," Ace groans when he notices my movement. His hand trails down my stomach and under the lip of my jeans. He plunges his hand down under my panties to test the wetness between my legs, drawing in a hiss when his finger makes contact with the moisture there.

"Tell me you don't want me," he whispers in my ear. "Tell me to stop, and I will."

I open my mouth, knowing that I should do just that, but no words come out. I can't fucking say them.

Because right now in this moment, I don't want him to stop. God, I don't want him to stop.

He must decide that me not stopping him isn't good enough, though, because he suddenly pulls back from me, lifting his head so that he can look right into my eyes.

Both of his hands are firmly planted on my hips now, and I feel my own wetness against my skin where he's gripping me with the finger he just had between my legs.

"Tell me you want this."

I clamp my lips together and just look up at him. I can't tell him to stop, but I don't know if I have the courage to admit that I want him either.

His jaw hardens, and his nostrils flare as his golden

eyes blaze down at me. "Your little pussy is weeping for me, but I want to hear you acknowledge that you want me. I'm not going to let you let this happen without you admitting that you want this too. You're not going to have an excuse to lump me into that group with every other man in the world."

He shakes his head as he goes on, "That's not us, Candace. We're more than that. I'm not just some guy from the club who wants to fuck you. I want you. All of you. Not just your body."

He licks his lips before he eyes settle on my lips again. "And once I fuck you, you're mine. You need to understand that." He drags his eyes away from my lips and back up to my meet my eyes. "There will be no going back. So, I ask you again, do you want this?"

I stare up at him, my heart pounding so loudly in my ears I'm surprised I can even make out what he said. He's right. My pussy is throbbing and wetter than I've ever been in my life. But is he also right that that's what I'm doing? Trying to make it so I have a cop-out for afterward, so that I can't try to convince myself I didn't really want this and that Ace isn't any different from all the men who ogled me at the club?

If I agree to this, I'm going in knowing full well that I'm giving myself to him. I won't be able to pretend that he took this from me. He's going to make me admit that I want this, or it won't happen.

He's perfectly still as he waits for my answer. Every muscle in his body is taut as his chest rises and falls with his labored breathing. It's obviously taking everything in him to hold back.

But he's doing it. And suddenly I know that if I do say no, he really will stop. As much as it might physically pain him to do so, he won't force me.

Ace is a man of his word, and he's proven that to me time and time again.

But he also hasn't lied to me and tried to pretend he's something he's not. He's never denied wanting me. In fact, he's made it very clear how much he does want me.

But he's leaving it up to me.

I have a choice.

So for once in my life, I think about what *I* really want. Not what I have to do or what I should do.

But what *I* want.

I take a deep breath and then give him my answer.

chapter
four

Ace

I'M WOUND up tighter than a spring as I wait for Candace's answer. God, I pray that she admits what's between us and that she wants this. I know that I could have taken her without a protest even without the admission, but I'm in this for the long haul. I'm not going to let her demonize me later on in her head.

I need her to face her feelings now and make a conscious decision.

I know Candy. She's fiercely independent. Whether she realizes it or not, she needs to know this was her decision. I figure she's been stripped of too many choices in her short life, forced into situations she never would have chosen for herself, and I'll be damned if I'm going to be like every other man in her life and impose my will on her without making sure it's what she wants.

Yes, her body tells me it's what she wants, but I need that beautiful mind of hers to catch up too.

Because I wasn't lying to her. I want to possess all of her: heart, mind, body, and soul. And once I get a taste of her, I know I'm going to be done for. There will be no stopping the possessive beast that rears its head.

She's silent for so long, I'm dreading she's going to say no. And then I will have to get far the fuck away from her to stay true to my word because my mother-fucking cock is about to bust through my boxers. I'm harder than the steel bar I was just lifting.

"Yes," she finally answers, her voice barely more than a whisper.

I cock my head down at her, wanting to be sure I've heard her correctly before I slacken the tight leash I have on myself.

She peeks up at me from underneath those long lashes, her cheeks pinkening prettily as she clears her throat and says louder, "Yes, Ace, I want this."

That's all I need to hear. "Thank fuck," I mutter as I drag her flush against me, letting her feel exactly what she does to me. I taste her lips again because, fuck, once was not enough. I could feast on her sweet lips for the rest of my life.

But there's something else I've been dying to taste, and now that I finally have her permission, I'm not going to deny myself any longer.

She yelps as I hoist her up in my arms and carry her over to my weight bench. I sit her on the bench and pull her shirt off, marveling at the perfect little mounds that are her breasts. I waste no time in sucking them into my mouth, swirling my tongue along the hardened peaks and delighting in the way her head falls back as she moans. Her hair brushes along my knuckles where I'm holding her firmly by the hips.

I try to pay her nipples plenty of attention, but I'm dying to unwrap the candy between her legs to get to her sweet core.

And I don't deny myself any longer. I work on pulling her pants down as I kiss my way across her stomach. She shivers underneath my touch and buries her fingers in my hair. Fuck, her little hands spearing through my strands feel like heaven. I'm like a feral dog that she's tamed with one touch. I find myself arching up into her touch, dying for more.

Fuck, what this little girl does to me. I knew it the first moment I saw her, that she was something special, something *mine*.

"Open those pretty little legs up for me, sweetheart," I tell her, my voice coming out husky as I kiss and lick the insides of her thighs. Damn, I can smell her already. She smells fucking incredible. I breathe in deeply, scenting my mate.

"Ace," her voice wobbles, but she does as I say.

I kiss her wet flesh, and she sucks in a breath. "Shh," I soothe her, blowing on her swollen clit.

She whimpers and tries to scramble away from me, but I hold her still.

"Been dying for a taste of this candy, baby," I tell her, practically salivating in anticipation.

I finally get my first taste, laving my tongue right up her center from her asshole up to her clit.

Fucking sugar. Pure fucking sugar. She's sweeter than any candy I've ever tasted. The real deal. Nirvana. I could die right now and be a happy man. I've tasted the promise land. Milk and honey has nothing on my girl.

My girl.

That thought fills me with purpose, and I begin to lap at her in earnest.

She mewls and moans and purrs. God, the sounds she makes are enough to make me nut. My cock is leaking a steady stream of precum, demanding release, but I ignore my own discomfort for now, intent on making my girl come.

I push a finger into her, marveling at how tight she is. I damn near lose it when I reach the barrier of her innocence and realize she's a virgin.

Fuck me, she's going to be completely mine. I'd want her regardless, but the thought that she's never been with another man before fills me with such a rush of pleasure I almost spill right there. I suction onto her clit, swirling my tongue over it in a figure eight, and she clenches her legs around my head, screaming as she orgasms.

I feel her pussy quaking around my finger, sucking at it greedily, and I can't wait to feel it doing that on my cock.

"Ace!" she screams my name, and I lose it.

I yank down my boxers, groaning as my swollen staff bobs free. "Yes, that's it, baby. You scream out my name when you come. Only mine."

She's still in the throes of her orgasm when I thrust myself inside her, burying myself inside her as deep as I can get, breaking through her hymen as quickly as I can to try to abate any pain I know she'll likely feel.

She screams and clings to me, her nails digging into my back like claws, but I don't care. I'm too high off the feeling of her little arms wrapped around me as she presses herself into me, holding onto me like I'm her lifeline. Yes, baby, I'll be your everything and more if you just let me.

Her pussy is so tight I don't even make it halfway inside her. She's squeezing me so tightly, my eyes threaten to roll back in my head. I blow out a breath and try to stay still long enough for her to adjust to me. "You okay, baby?" I ask her through gritted teeth.

"Yes," she finally says breathlessly, and I test the truth in her statement by pulling out a fraction of an inch and pushing back inside her, sinking deeper into her this time.

She moans and clutches at me harder, her pussy tightening around me. "Is it all the way in?" she asks me.

I let out a chuckle and kiss her lips. "No, baby, I still got more to give you."

Her eyes widen, and I pull out and push back in again, sinking even further inside her.

She moans and tosses her head back.

Sweat is breaking out on my brow. It's costing me to hold back like this, but I can do this for her. "Feel good?" I ask her, my brow furrowed. God, it feels fucking incredible to me, but I can't stand the thought that I'm hurting her.

Her light brown eyes are wide, but they flutter closed as she answers, "Yes, feels so good. Don't stop."

I can't stop the guttural groan that rips from my chest as I start surging deeper inside her until I finally have her pulsing around my entire length.

"That little pussy is mine, isn't it, baby?" I ask her desperately as I continue to move within her. Fuck, I can't sit still now. *Claim, claim, claim.* My body is responding to my instincts. I move my hands to cup either side of her face, forcing her to look at me. "Let me see those eyes, sweetheart."

She snaps them open and bites her bottom lip as she stares up at me. "Ace," she whimpers, and I groan, bending down to bite that lip myself as I continue plowing into her, tingles already racing up my spine.

My balls feel so motherfucking heavy. They're churning and drawing up, and I know I'll be popping off any moment.

"Fuck, Candace. Give it to me, baby," I urge her, needing to feel her little pussy falling open around me when I bust in her.

I feel myself swelling inside her and jab her hard and deep two more times. "Come on, baby," I beg her. I hastily lick my thumb and then press it down on her clit, and thank fuck, she detonates with a screech of my name.

Hearing her scream my name while she comes with my cock deep inside her is enough to tip me right over the edge.

I feel her pussy spasming around me just as I feel the

rush of my release surging up my stalk and toward my tip.

I hold it back for as long as I can, just enjoying the feeling of her muscles contracting around me, milking me for all I'm worth, until I can't hold it anymore and finally let loose, jets of sperm tearing from my body and spraying up into her.

"Motherfucking damn it!" I shout as my sperm floods her. I've never bust such a big nut in my entire life, and I feel like I might pass out. I'm still moving inside her jerkily, prolonging both of our release until I'm spilling out around her. Her thighs and my balls are sticky and wet, and I'm panting above her, struggling to keep from toppling over. Somehow, I manage to pull her into my arms with my cock still inside her and spin us so that I'm lying on the bench with her cradled against my chest.

I stroke her hair down her back and kiss the top of her head, content to hold her in my arms like this for the rest of our lives.

Mine. She's mine now.

chapter
five

Candy

I LAY on Ace's chest for the longest time, loving the feeling of the rise and fall of his breathing. He pets my hair, and I stay curled up on him like a cat basking in her master's affection. I never thought sex could be so...fulfilling.

It wasn't dirty or painful like a lot of the other strippers where I worked made it out to be. Yes, there was a bit of discomfort at first, but it quickly morphed into the most intense pleasure.

And this...I snuggle deeper into his chest...having

him hold me afterward like this, like I'm the most precious thing in his entire world. This is nice.

He tightens his arms around me and continues stroking me for a while as we just lay in each other's arms and breathe together.

His cock eventually slips out of me and he breathes a question against my hair.

"You hungry, baby?"

I look up at him, and my tummy chooses that moment to answer for me with a loud growl.

He chuckles, the rumble resonating through my own chest where it's pressed against his.

I grin and admit, "I could go for a pizza."

"Pizza it is then, sweetheart. Just let me go grab my phone from my office."

I push up off him and stay him with my hand. "It's okay. I can run and get it for you."

He settles back down on the bench with his hands behind his head, unabashedly naked and taking in the view of my naked body as well.

I try not to drool at the sight of him spread out on his exercise equipment that way, the girth and length of his flaccid cock still more impressive than some fully erect ones.

He smirks when he catches me gazing at him, and my cheeks heat. I hurry to put on my clothes. "Be right back," I chirp before I head for his office to retrieve his phone for him.

I spot it sitting on his desk. As I reach out to pick it up, my hand hits his mouse, causing his computer screen to light up.

My eyes flick up to the screen, and I see something that gives me pause.

I'm normally not one to snoop through other people's belongings, but there's a file on his desktop with my name on it.

My curiosity gets the best of me, and I figure if it has *my* name on it, I have the right to know what's in it, so I click on the folder labeled "Candace."

My eyes widen and my heart falls to my stomach when I register what I'm looking at.

It's a wire transfer for an insane amount of money. To Dan. My stepdad.

Tears flood my eyes as I realize this only means one thing.

Ace *bought* me. He bought me like I'm just some material thing.

All this time I thought he was different, that he was really offering me a new life just out of the kindness of his heart. That he actually *cared* about me. That he didn't just want me for what he could get out of me.

When all along, I was just another *thing* to him. My

mind goes back to that day he approached me in the club. He made it sound like he was offering me a new life. He said not to worry about Dan, that he'd take care of him. Was he only so confident because he'd already worked out a deal with Dan to take me off his hands?

Was all of this just one elaborate trick to make me think that I really had a choice when I never did? Because if he'd bought me, I was his, right? He could technically make me do whatever he wanted. He owned me. I owed him my life. Literally.

The tears stream down my cheeks. This cuts too fucking deep. I opened myself up to him. Gave myself to him. And then I find out that he's just like all the other men who go to Dan's club. Why the fuck am I surprised? Of course he is. Otherwise, what was he doing there to begin with?

Well, fuck him. I wipe at my tears angrily. I'm not going to be owned. He got what he paid for, right? Sex and candy.

I'm sure he won't care if I jet now, and frankly, I don't give a fuck if he does.

I can't bear to look him in the eyes ever again.

I don't even bother to gather any of my belongings except my phone. It's the only thing I had that was truly mine before I came here, so it's all I take with me. All my new clothes and everything else was bought with Ace's money, and I'll be damned if I take anything from him.

I slip out of his upscale townhouse as quickly as I can and take off walking.

I should have fucking known better. No man ever does anything for free.

———

Ace

I think I feel the exact moment she leaves. Suddenly, my entire body feels cold, and something just tells me that something's wrong. I throw on my clothes and hurry into my office to see what's taking her so long, praying that she somehow just got sidetracked and that my instincts are off.

But my instincts are never off, and it doesn't take me long to figure out what happened.

My cell phone is still laying untouched on the desk, but my computer screen is lit up with a copy of the wire transfer I sent Dan displayed on the screen.

Candy must have seen that and deduced what happened, that I essentially bought her from Dan. And I know she's not okay with that. I can see her eyes flashing fire now.

So my girl ran.

Fuck!

I spear my fingers into my hair and pull tight, panic clawing at my chest. I finally had her. She gave herself to me of her own free will, and now it's all going to be fucked up.

I begin to pace my office, my mind going a mile a minute. Where the fuck would she go? Surely she wouldn't go back to Dan?

My eyes flit across my office and I nearly sag with relief when I don't see her phone on her own desk.

Maybe there really is a God and he's throwing me a bone because if she's got her phone with her, then I can track her.

I'm on my phone in a heartbeat, calling my man to get the location on Candace's phone.

I don't give a fuck how mad she is at me. I have to explain this to her, and I meant what I said.

When she gave herself to me, she agreed to be mine, and I'm not going to lose her now.

chapter
six

Candy

I DON'T KNOW how long I wander the city streets alone before I realize that it's getting dark, and I don't have anywhere to go.

I look up at the first sign I see and harden my jaw when I see that I'm standing right outside Dan's biggest rival.

I don't really know anything about this club other than my stepdad always hated the owner. They were always in competition to see who could get the most business, and something bitter takes residence inside me at the thought of helping pull business away from my slimy stepfather.

Fuck him and fuck Ace.

I hesitate a moment, the thought of going back on the pole making me want to eat nails instead. But then I flush with humiliation when I remember how I gave myself to Ace only to turn around and find out that he'd bought me like so much meat.

This is obviously all I'm good for. So I might as well get paid for it.

I'm under no illusions that the owner of this club will give me the same special treatment that Dan did, though I'm sure Dan didn't do it out of any sentimentality for me or my dead mother.

No, he was protecting his investment. Just how long did he have planned to sell me off for? I definitely think he knew I was a virgin now because why else would a man pay that much for a woman? And why else would Dan have been so adamant about not letting anyone touch me?

My stomach quakes at the thought of letting another man touch me, though. I don't know if I can do it. Surely, I won't have to sleep with them, though. Maybe I can get away with just doing lap dances.

I bite my lip, indecision warring inside my body as I hover outside the door. Just as I decide not to go in, the door swings open, and a burly-looking man fills the doorframe.

He towers over me, his face morphing into a smile when he sees me standing there like a mouse that's wandered right into the cat's den.

"Well, well, well. What do we have here?" he says, his gaze roving over my body lasciviously.

I take a step backward, and he tuts at me. "Where are you going, little mouse? No need to be shy. Hey," he assesses me again, recognition lighting his eyes, "aren't you Dan's little bird?"

My throat goes dry as I shake my head, but it's too late. I've already been caught.

I turn around to run, but I feel his large arm snake around my middle, pulling me back into him. "Why don't you come on in and stay a while, sweetheart?" I can smell his stale breath from here, and the stench is nauseating. Hearing the same endearment Ace used for me dripping from this man's lips causes my heart to wrench within my chest.

I'm suddenly wishing I hadn't left Ace's. Maybe I overreacted after all. Maybe he had a good explanation for the money wired to Dan.

In any case, Ace wasn't as bad as this man. I can feel the evil dripping off of him.

"I really have someplace to be," I tell him, internally

cursing myself when my voice comes out sounding shaky and weak.

"Of course you do," he says placatingly as he pulls me through the door. "I've got the perfect spot for you. With an ass like that, you'll be my biggest money maker, and it's you're lucky day. I just so happen to have a room open, and it's all yours now, sweetheart. Of course, I get to be the first one to sample the merchandise." He chuckles at his own stipulation as he pulls me through the darkened corridor.

I pull against his hand, trying to free myself. "No, you're making a mistake. I'm not looking for work. I already have a job."

He just laughs harder as he ignores me and continues pulling me along.

Panic begins to claw at my chest. Something tells me this man isn't even going to pretend to give me a choice.

I begin to fight against him in earnest, kicking and clawing at him now.

His face contorts into a mask of rage when my foot makes contact with his shin. "You're gonna pay for that, you little bitch," he hisses at me as he pulls a hand back to strike me.

I wince in preparation for the hit, but it never comes.

An inhuman roar sounds behind me, and I glance over my shoulder to see Ace barreling through the door.

He grabs the man's raised hand and bends it back. I hear snapping, and the man screams as Ace breaks bone. "Keep your motherfucking hands off my girl!" Ace snarls at him before he knocks him out cold.

I'm frozen to the spot, staring with wide eyes at Ace. He turns to me, his body still vibrating with fury. His eyes soften, though, when they land on me, and I hate myself for it, but I burst into tears.

"Sshh, come here, baby. I've got you," he tells me as he gathers me into his arms. I go willingly, wrapping my arms and legs around him and allowing him to carry me out in his arms chimp-style.

I bury my face in his neck and breathe in his comforting scent. He strokes my hair as he tells me, "Nothing is ever going to hurt you again. Including me, baby. It's not what you think."

I look up at him and sniff, "You mean you didn't buy my virginity?"

His jaw hardens as he shakes his head, "No, I just paid Dan off to avoid having to kill a bunch of mother-fuckers, but I never viewed it as buying you. You've always had a choice with me. I wouldn't ever make you do anything you didn't want to do."

"So, if I want to leave now you'll let me?" I ask him with a raised eyebrow.

His expression sours and he looks torn. "Do you want to leave?" he asks me warily.

I consider lying and tell him yes just to see what he'll say, but he looks so miserable, I find myself telling him the truth instead. "No," I admit. "I want to stay with you."

He expels a relieved breath. "Thank fuck because I don't think I could really let you go, honey. I think I could give you time, but I'd always be there in the background waiting for the moment you needed me. I couldn't let you just go off unprotected. I won't lie to you about that."

The ardent way he makes his admission has my heart melting. Ace may have gone about it wrong, but that doesn't mean that he doesn't truly care for me.

I place my hands on either side of his face and look into his eyes. "I never did get that pizza," I say seriously.

He throws his head back and laughs, a booming sound that brings a smile to my face.

"Why don't we stop by the pizzeria on the way home and dine in?" he suggests.

My tummy growls, and I nod.

He laughs again. "Come on. Let me feed my baby."

He carries me all the way to the pizzeria, completely oblivious to the looks from passersby. Some girls swoon, some mothers roll their eyes, and some men have knowing grins on their faces.

We ignore them all.

Ace doesn't set me down until he places me in the booth at the restaurant and slides in next to me instead of sitting across from me.

And I realize that this is exactly where I choose to be.

Beside Ace.

epilogue

Three Years Later

Ace

I **WALK** through the front door of my wife's studio and stand in the corner, openly watching her as she instructs her class of preteens.

She's doing what she loves, teaching promising students how to safely do gymnastics and go for the gold. One of her students just last year went to the Olympics, and Candace couldn't have been prouder.

I hate that she never got to perform in the Olympics

herself. No doubt she'd have won, but she insists that she's right where she's meant to be.

With me and our two children. It didn't take me a month to have Candace knocked up, and it's no wonder with my aversion to condoms. There's never going to be anything between my wife and me.

Never.

And I balked at the thought of her putting any chemicals in her body that blocked my sperm from doing their job. We had a conversation about it, and thank god, she didn't insist on taking birth control. Of course, part of that could have been due to the fact that by the time we got around to having the conversation she was already pregnant. In fact, I'm almost certain I got her pregnant with that first big nut I bust in her the day she gave herself to me, but that's neither here nor there.

She let me fund her studio, and my business is lucrative enough that I can still conduct business from home and have plenty of time to spend with my girls.

Molly and Mary are our pride and joy. They both look just like their mother, though Mary has my darker coloring. I'll probably go to prison when they get old enough to start dating. Candace laughs when I make comments like that, but I'm not motherfucking playing.

I'll kill some fuckers for hurting my princesses. Any of them, my wife included.

Right now, our three-year-old and one-year-old are with their nanny while Mommy and Daddy work. Well, Daddy decided to go ahead and call it a day and come pick Mommy up from work because he's been too long without her.

I watch as Candace does a few flips, her execution flawless, her ass looking like a ripe peach in those skintight yoga pants she's wearing. Good thing there's no men signed up to her classes. I'd have to murder some motherfuckers because no man in his right mind would be able to keep his eyes off that ass.

She straightens and then walks around the room, correcting a few girls' posture and giving them instructions on what to practice before she dismisses them from class.

The moment she spots me watching her, she graces me with a radiant smile. Little wisps of hair have escaped her ponytail and frame her face.

Fuck, I'm the luckiest son of a bitch on this planet.

I walk over to her as her students begin to file out of the studio, waving goodbye to her.

"Why aren't you at work?" she asks me with a raised eyebrow.

I grin down at her as I capture her waist in my hands. "I thought I'd come by and help you with your stretching."

She grins up at me. "You want to help me with my cool down?"

"No way, sweetheart," I shake my head at her before I lean down and say right against her ear, "I want to help you warm up."

A shiver passes through her, and I feel my cock jerk in my slacks in response.

"Plus, I'm craving something sweet," I croon at her. I'm always hungry for the sugar between my wife's legs. I can't go a day without eating her. I swear to God I can't.

Just as I bend down to kiss her lips, she dodges me, falling to her knees and pulling my cock from my slacks.

"Oh, fuck me," I groan out as her hot, little mouth wraps around my swollen length. She's instantly hollowing her cheeks and sucking me back deep, swirling her tongue along the underside of my tip in that way that drives me motherfucking crazy.

It's just fucking like her to try to take control of the situation and drive me to my knees. My little Candy loves nothing more than having me in the palm of her hand.

I twirl her hair around my fist and hold on. I let her slurp on my dick for a solid minute before I jerk her to her feet and yank her yoga pants down to her knees. Quick as lightning, I lift her and flip her over, holding her so that she's upside down, her sweet pussy right in my face. She doesn't weigh more than a feather, and I love holding her upside down and eating her out this way.

I don't waste any time diving in to my favorite treat, and I feel her hot mouth envelop me again.

She's bobbing her head back and forth on me as much as she can while I thrust my tongue deep into her wet folds.

I can tell she's close to coming, so I suck hard on her clit. I'm rewarded when she screams around my cock and gushes cream into my mouth.

The vibrations of her moaning with my dick halfway down her throat have me coming too. I push my cock as far back in her throat as I can get it before I release my seed into her waiting mouth.

We keep eating each other out until I feel her arms go lax around where she's holding my legs.

I gently turn her back upright and then kiss her lips, licking at her mouth, letting the taste of us combine together.

She twines her tongue with mine, kissing me back, and I already feel my cock hardening again.

"Did you get what you came for?" she whispers huskily against my lips.

"I sure did. Best fucking candy I ever tasted."
But I'm not fucking done with her.
I'll never be done with her.

THE END

Want more books by Emma Bray?

Check out her Amazon page.